D1636305

Bantam Books in the Choose Your Own Adventure Series
Ask your bookseller for the books you have missed

#1 THE CAVE OF TIME
#2 JOURNEY UNDER THE SEA
#3 DANGER IN THE DESERT
#4 SPACE AND BEYOND
#5 THE CURSE OF THE
  HAUNTED MANSION
#6 SPY TRAP
#7 MESSAGE FROM SPACE
#8 DEADWOOD CITY
#9 WHO KILLED HARLOWE
  THROMBEY?
#10 THE LOST JEWELS
#22 SPACE PATROL
#31 VAMPIRE EXPRESS
#52 GHOST HUNTER
#58 STATUE OF LIBERTY
  ADVENTURE
#63 MYSTERY OF THE SECRET
  ROOM
#66 SECRET OF THE NINJA
#70 INVADERS OF THE PLANET
  EARTH
#71 SPACE VAMPIRE
#72 THE BRILLIANT DR. WOGAN
#73 BEYOND THE GREAT WALL
#74 LONGHORN TERRITORY
#75 PLANET OF THE DRAGONS
#76 THE MONA LISA IS MISSING!
#77 THE FIRST OLYMPICS

#78 RETURN TO ATLANTIS
#79 MYSTERY OF THE SACRED
  STONES
#80 THE PERFECT PLANET
#81 TERROR IN AUSTRALIA
#82 HURRICANE!
#83 TRACK OF THE BEAR
#84 YOU ARE A MONSTER
#85 INCA GOLD
#86 KNIGHTS OF THE ROUND
  TABLE
#87 EXILED TO EARTH
#88 MASTER OF KUNG FU
#89 SOUTH POLE SABOTAGE
#90 MUTINY IN SPACE
#91 YOU ARE A SUPERSTAR
#92 RETURN OF THE NINJA
#93 CAPTIVE!
#94 BLOOD ON THE HANDLE
#95 YOU ARE A GENIUS
#96 STOCK CAR CHAMPION
#97 THROUGH THE BLACK HOLE
#98 YOU ARE A MILLIONAIRE
#99 REVENGE OF THE RUSSIAN
  GHOST (Mar.)
#100 THE WORST DAY OF YOUR
  LIFE (Apr.)
#101 ALIEN, GO HOME! (May)
#102 MASTER OF TAE KWON DO
  (June)

#1 JOURNEY TO THE YEAR 3000 (A Choose Your Own Adventure Super Adventure)
#2 DANGER ZONES (A Choose Your Own Adventure Super Adventure)

YOU ARE A SUPERSTAR

BY EDWARD PACKARD

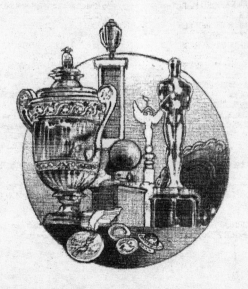

ILLUSTRATED BY STEPHEN MARCHESI

BANTAM BOOKS

NEW YORK · TORONTO · LONDON · SYDNEY · AUCKLAND

RL 5, IL age 10 and up

YOU ARE A SUPERSTAR
A Bantam Book / May 1989

*CHOOSE YOUR OWN ADVENTURE® is a registered trademark of
Bantam Books, a division of Bantam Doubleday Dell Publishing
Group, Inc. Registered in U.S. Patent and Trademark Office
and elsewhere.*

Original conception of Edward Packard

*Cover art by Catherine Huerta
Interior illustrations by Stephen Marchesi*

ISBN 0-553-27913-0

Published simultaneously in the United States and Canada

Bantam Books are published by Bantam Books, a division of Bantam Doubleday
Dell Publishing Group, Inc. Its trademark, consisting of the words "Bantam
Books" and the portrayal of a rooster, is Registered in U.S. Patent and Trademark
Office and in other countries. Marca Registrada. Bantam Books, 666 Fifth Ave-
nue, New York, New York 10103.

PRINTED IN THE UNITED STATES OF AMERICA

O   0 9 8 7 6 5

YOU ARE A
SUPERSTAR

WARNING!!!

Do not read this book straight through from beginning to end. These pages contain many different adventures that you may have as you focus your talents and become a superstar. As you read, you will be able to make a choice. Your choice will lead to either stardom or failure!

Each adventure you take is the result of your choice. You are responsible because you choose! After you make a choice, follow the instructions to see what happens to you next.

Think carefully before you make a decision. Being a superstar is not always glamorous and exciting. Sometimes success can turn your victories into disasters!

Good luck!

You've always been pretty good at sports. You've played quite a bit of baseball, a little tennis, and you're a fast runner. You're not a bad swimmer either. In fact it's while you're swimming one day that you first notice something strange happening to your body. Not that you start looking different. It's something you can feel inside.

The municipal pool is quite long—twenty-five yards—and one of your goals for quite a while has been to swim the whole length underwater. It's Saturday morning. The pool has just opened, and there are only a couple of other swimmers in the water. You have a whole lane for yourself, so you take a couple of deep breaths and dive in. *Swoosh, swoosh, swoosh* . . . you glide underwater.

This is the time I'm going to make it, you think!

Suddenly you see the wall at the end of the pool a few feet away, but, amazingly, you don't feel the slightest bit out of breath! Still underwater, you push off the wall and start another lap, never imagining that you'll get all the way back to the other end of the pool, but you do! Not only do you make it, but you're still not tired or out of breath. You push off to swim the length of the pool again! It feels great and also kind of weird, as you stroke and glide far more smoothly than you ever have before.

Turn to page 10.

Again the pitch comes in, and you can see the ball clearly, every inch of the way. It's going to pass outside the strike zone—a couple of inches high and maybe four or five inches outside—but you know you can hit it. You swing, and it's a line drive, right over the second baseman's head. You take off down the baseline, turning on the speed, your eye on the right fielder, who catches the ball on one hop. Normally that would mean holding at first, but you've already crossed the bag and are doing a wide turn. You head for second, putting on a terrific burst of speed. You don't look over your shoulder, but you can almost sense that the right fielder is throwing the ball to the shortstop, covering second. You get ready to slide, but then, realizing how fast you're running, you just keep going!

You run right over the bag, and you're almost halfway to third when you hear the ball land in the shortstop's mitt. By now you can't stop. You round third, again ahead of the ball, and run for home! You're only halfway there when you see the ball fly over your head and into the catcher's mitt.

Go on to the next page.

Grimes, the catcher, walks toward you with the ball in his strong right hand. You know the third baseman's closing in from behind—they're going to try to run you down. You stop short and take a step toward third. Grimes is getting ready to throw. As the ball leaves his fingers, you're racing for home! With a tremendous leap you slide headfirst. Your hand touches the plate half a second before Grimes slaps you with his mitt.

Safe!

The crowd goes wild! Everyone is cheering and yelling. No one's ever seen anything like it! Something amazing has happened.

Turn to page 14.

In the past you hadn't given much thought to going into politics, but the more you think about running for Congress, the more you like the idea, particularly because you'll be fighting against Martin Beowulf, the veteran political boss who has ruled in your district for so many years. Beowulf has been able to keep power by getting a lot of government contracts for a couple of big companies in the area. But he has done nothing to clean up pollution, he's blocked funds for better schools, and he's wasted a lot of the taxpayers' money. Basically, he's a rat.

You know he'll be hard to beat—he's tough and he's ruthless. But you wage a good, hard, honest campaign. After the election you're up all night while the returns are counted. At last the vote is in. You lost. Crafty old Beowulf got just 51.4 percent of the votes, and you got 48.6 percent.

You feel bad, but to your surprise, lots of people call to congratulate you. Everyone says that you did very well considering it was your first time out against a powerful party boss.

The governor himself calls you just before you're going home for the night.

"That was a great race you ran," he says.

"I wish I could feel good about it," you say.

"You've got a great future," the governor says. "Just remember: even superstars don't always win the first time."

The End

6

On your return from the tour, you sleep all afternoon, and at 6 p.m. report to the auditorium where The Syndrome is going to perform for the highest-level officials of the Communist Party. Popovitch, the foreign minister, is there and also Pyotyr Glandinowsky, the minister of culture. He explains to you that rock music used to be considered a bad influence on the Russian youth—but lately things have changed.

"Don't trust these guys," Kenny whispers to you later. "They want to *use* you."

You decide that you won't trust them, and you won't *not* trust them either. You'll just sing your heart out. The rest of the group does the same. When you sing your "trademark" number, "Breakdown on the Line," at the end of the show, the normally well-disciplined members of the Communist Progressive Youth Workers of the USSR start cheering and yelling uncontrollably. You're afraid they've gone too far, but then you see Secretary Popovitch and Minister Glandinowsky also standing and cheering. You glance at the side aisles where the KGB men are watching. Even these guys are clapping and smiling.

Most exciting, right after the show, you get a call from the secretary general.

Turn to page 108.

"Hi," he answers back. "I've been listening to a few of The Syndrome records lately—some of the songs you wrote in particular—and I've got to tell you I haven't heard anything like this since Elvis Presley. Frankly I like your stuff a lot better. It's multichromatic!"

Multichromatic? You'd never thought of your music that way.

"You've not only been making great music," he says, "you've been showing your concern for people and problems, and not just thinking of your own comfort and glory."

"Well, thank you, sir." You're beginning to wonder what this is leading up to.

"So I hope you'll be willing to do something very important for our country," he continues.

"Gosh, what do you have in mind, Mr. President?"

"I'd like it if The Syndrome would do a tour of Russia. We've gotten feelers that the new premier there, the secretary general, is a fancier of your records, or at least his kids are. And we think we could line up a major tour through our State Department. The Soviets could hardly refuse because of their policy of *glasnost*—or openness. They're anxious to prove to the world that they are not a closed and secretive society the way they used to be."

"I catch your drift, Mr. President."

"Good—so let me know if you'll do it, and I'll set things in motion."

Turn to page 43.

"I can't believe it!" Ms. Tignor exclaims. She looks at the picture, then at you, then back at the picture again. "It's a masterpiece!" Then she frowns. "Did you *really* do this?"

"I sure did, Ms. Tignor. First I did a sketch for it—I wish I'd brought it along."

Ms. Tignor looks skeptically at you. "I know you have talent, and this work certainly looks as fresh as an original. Still—it's hard to believe that you could suddenly turn out such a great work."

"Watch this," you say. While Ms. Tignor watches, you take out a sheet of paper and draw another tiger, this one rearing up dramatically on its hind legs.

Ms. Tignor gasps as she sees how quickly and adroitly you draw it. "You have great, great talent," she says. "You are a true artist."

With Ms. Tignor's help you get a full scholarship to the Kenworth Academy of Fine Arts—the art academy where some of America's greatest artists have studied. There you're able to realize your passion for art of all kinds. You do oils, acrylics, watercolors, and sculpture. For your first show, you do some large wood carvings of animals, and in the following term you make woodcuts and etchings. But your real love is painting. You do huge paintings—scenes of crowds, whole forest scenes filled with birds and animals and shimmering light. People stand for half an hour in front of some of your paintings!

Turn to page 24.

As you start your fourth lap, you're finally beginning to feel the need for air. You keep pushing along, and you make it. You've just swum a hundred yards, all underwater!

When you finally surface, the lifeguard is standing at the end of the pool staring at you. "Hey, that was some swimming! I thought you'd turned into a fish!"

The other swimmers are hanging on to the edge of the pool staring at you too. They can't believe it. Nobody is more surprised than you. You quit for the day, and you don't even brag about what you've done. That night you go to bed feeling pretty good, but also a little spooked. It was all so strange—you can't help but wonder what's going on.

The next day when you play baseball you have an odd sensation. You're up at bat, and you watch the ball coming in toward the plate. You can *see* it moving—see the stitches turning almost as if the ball were coming toward you in slow motion. You've never been able to see a ball like that before. You're so surprised that you forget to swing.

Turn to page 2.

The group is invited to play everywhere—Carnegie Hall, the White House—you name it. One day you pick up the *New York Times* and read on the front page, "Ginger Blue and The Syndrome are a national frenzy." Then you know it's got to be true!

It's a lot of fun even though you're only a superstar and Ginger Blue is a super superstar. After all, you're not vain.

The End

12

"I think most of all I'd like to be a track star—a runner," you say. "I'd like to be the world's fastest human."

"Good." Dr. Ruddick is obviously pleased—he was a long-distance runner himself in college and came pretty close to doing a 4-minute mile.

Your mom walks over and gives you a pat on the shoulder. "Just remember to keep up your schoolwork. You'll want to sound intelligent when they interview you on the talk shows."

The years pass swiftly. Before you know it you're in high school. The track coach is beside himself with joy at having you on the team. Everyone's eyes are upon you as you quickly break all the school records, running the 100-yard dash in 9.8 seconds and the 110-yard high hurdles in 13 flat.

Of course, your picture is in the local papers, and you're even mentioned by a couple of sportscasters on national TV. You're only a freshman in high school at this point, and people are expecting big things from you.

And you're expecting big things from yourself. Some day, you're certain, you're going to be in the Olympics!

Turn to page 74.

You decide that Sheldon is right. Your fans won't expect you to actually skate in the film, they'll want to see you act.

Unfortunately this doesn't turn out to be true. After months of grueling work shooting the movie, you realize that you're not a very good actor and the real star of the picture is the skater. When word gets out that you aren't doing the work but are getting the credit and the money, lots of your fans turn on you. You start getting hundreds of letters a week from angry fans who call you a phony, a cheat, and a jerk.

Despite it all, the film is a great success at the box office. Thanks to the deal you made with Sheldon, you're richer than you'd ever imagined. But money can't buy back the respect of your fans, or yourself. You realize there isn't a future for you in film, and now you're just a superstar has-been.

The End

14

From that moment on your life is changed. You discover you've become a super athlete, and no matter what sport you compete in—including a few you hadn't tried before, like soccer and gymnastics—you're better than anyone else. Every day you get faster and stronger.

Of course your parents are very pleased and proud, and your sister and brother are half pleased and proud and half jealous.

Your mom is a little afraid that you'll get so caught up in sports that you'll neglect your homework. "You don't want to grow up to be a great athlete who's a dumbbell," she says.

It's true that you don't have quite as much time for homework anymore. One reason is that you've taken up the piano. You've been at the keyboard a lot, trying to decide whether to become a jazz or pop pianist or to play classical music. The trouble is you're so good at both. You've also spent quite a bit of time drawing. You'd never realized you were so good at art.

About a year after it all started in the municipal swimming pool, your parents and you and Dr. Lyman Ruddick, who is not only your family medical advisor, but also a good friend, sit down to talk about your future.

"There seems to be little doubt about what's happened," Dr. Ruddick says. "You've undergone a very, very rare genetic mutation—one that has produced these marvelous changes in your body and your brain."

Turn to page 22.

You've played a little tennis and watched the top players on TV, and one year you had a chance to watch the U.S. Open. You're really hooked on tennis. It's fun, it's challenging, and you can play it almost anywhere. Track is OK, but you'd rather play a *game*! You just love swatting that tennis ball.

When you tell your parents you've decided to become a tennis pro, your dad says, "The best way to find out whether tennis is the sport for you is to go at it intensively."

You don't have any trouble following your dad's advice. You feel like playing tennis all the time. Every day that summer you play at the municipal courts. They have some pretty good tennis players there, and soon you're playing with the best of them. You get a great feeling as your strokes improve and you begin to develop a strong serve.

The next summer you go to a tennis camp run by Steve Chandler, who was a nationally ranked player for many years, won the French Open once, and was a runner-up at Wimbledon a couple of times. Steve wasn't the strongest player around in his day, but he understands the game as well as anyone. You feel really lucky to get into his camp.

Unfortunately Steve isn't around much of the time, but the other pros are pretty good, and your game improves rapidly. The main thing is that you've developed a really good ball sense.

Turn to page 96.

When you get to Hollywood, you meet with Sheldon Carver, the chief producer for Neptune Films. Sheldon has so much thick wavy gray hair on his head that you wonder if his barber charges extra to cut it. When he talks, which is most of the time, he waves a huge cigar around to emphasize his points. Fortunately he never seems to light it.

"We have a great movie for you to star in," he says. "It's about a champion figure skater whose skates are sabotaged by an unknown enemy. The movie turns into a spy story of sorts."

"How would I play a champion figure skater?" you interrupt. "That's not my sport. I'm not sure I would be good enough on the ice."

"Do you think most movie stars can really do what they seem to do on the screen?" Sheldon asks. "Remember, you're not being hired as a sports champion, but as an *actor*. Of course it will help if you skate well, and with your great athletic ability, I'm sure you'll look pretty good on the ice. For the really technical stuff we'll use special camera angles, fast motion, and a real champion skater to double for you."

"I don't know . . ." you say. "It seems sort of phony."

Sheldon's fist comes down on the table. "It's *not* phony! It's the movies. It's Hollywood."

If you decide to go along with Sheldon and let someone else do the skating, turn to page 13.

If you decide to argue with Sheldon until he lets you skate, turn to page 67.

You just keep piling on the speed, down the icy slope. You're sliding on ice, accelerating every second. There's no traction. You can't turn. Your skis are clattering wildly on the ice, your knees taking the shocks. The wind is a hurricane. *Your leg is sliding out. You're skiing on your left ski and knuckles!* You're up! Crouching again, driving— every meter . . . to the *finish!*

The crowd is roaring. The cameramen close in on you. Then you see your time posted on the board: 1:56.11—it's the best—almost a second better than the great Elsin Zrigrn!

You've won the gold. *You're a superstar!*

Turn to page 27.

When you return to the site of the missing painting, the alarm bell is still clanging, and the other guards are running around like headless chickens. Moments later you hear sirens outside. The police have arrived—too late, of course, to catch the thief.

It seems odd that the picture stolen was the only fake in the gallery. *Was it just a coincidence?* you wonder. *Or is there another explanation?*

Later that day, after the police have left, you decide to pay a call on Jason Marsden.

"I can only talk a minute," he says as you look in the door to his office. "I have a lot to do after that outrageous theft."

"I can understand," you say. "I just wanted you to know, since it might make a difference, that the painting that was stolen is a fake."

"What!" The director, red-faced with anger, is on his feet. "How dare you suggest such a thing! I examined that painting before the academy bought it. I wouldn't have let them pay over a million dollars for an *imitation!*" Marsden glares at you. "If you repeat this to anyone," he says, "you'll regret it. No one will believe you."

"Mr. Marsden," you say, "did you know that the painting was a fake?"

Marsden answers between clenched teeth. "If I did, would I have allowed the academy to spend a million dollars to buy it?"

You look him straight in the eye. "Perhaps you would—if you could keep the real one for yourself," you say.

Turn to page 25.

The fans are on the edge of their seats. You serve the next two points, but you fault on your first serve each point and only win one of them.

Blair serves, leading 4–3, serves deep. You smash it back and rush the net, stretch for the return, and put it away crosscourt. You smile at the crowd—you surprised Blair completely. Now you're on the offensive. You play like a demon, lunging for Blair's ground strokes and racing across the court to retrieve what look like winners.

Your serve at 5–4. Blair smashes the ball to your backhand. A long rally follows. Then he blasts the ball into a corner. You barely get your racket on it, but you get a drop shot over the net. Blair hits it deep to your backhand. As he rushes the net, you smash the ball down the line. Suddenly it's all over—you've won the tiebreaker 6–3 . . . Game . . . Set . . . Match!

The roar of the crowd drowns out the jet plane zooming overhead. You've won the U.S. Open— the Grand Slam! There's no doubt about it now— *you are a superstar!*

Turn to page 30.

"Mutation! What a horrible word," your mom gasps.

Dr. Ruddick nods. "Indeed, mutations are usually harmful. If a mutation in a fish caused it to have an extra fin, for example, the fish probably would not survive. The extra fin would be much more likely to cause problems than to help. But rarely, very rarely, a mutation changes an organism for the better. That's exactly what has happened to your child."

You gulp. "I sure feel lucky."

"You are lucky," says your dad. "The hard part is what to do with this incredible talent you've developed. Now you've got to spend some time thinking about what you want to be—what you want to accomplish."

"The fact is," says your mom, "it's just possible that you could become a superstar!"

Your dad looks you in the eye. "But what kind of a superstar do you want to be?" he asks.

With all of your super talents, it won't be an easy choice, but if you really want to be a superstar, you'll have to concentrate your energy on one thing at a time. What will it be?

Go on to the next page.

---

*If you decide to be a track star,
turn to page 12.*

*If you decide to be a baseball star,
turn to page 46.*

*If you decide to be a tennis star,
turn to page 16.*

*If you decide to be a skiing star,
turn to page 28.*

*If you decide to be a musician,
turn to page 111.*

If you decide to be an artist, turn to page 35.

*If you decide not to make up your mind just
now, turn to page 52.*

But one thing bothers you about the Kenworth Academy: there is a fake Picasso hanging in its collection titled *Garçon avec Cheval*. It's a picture of a boy standing next to a horse. It's a very clever fake—you can understand why most people would think the painting was genuine. But you notice telltale brush strokes around the boy's eyes that Picasso would never have made. It puzzles you that Jason Marsden, the director of the academy, hasn't noticed that the painting is a fake. He is one of the foremost Picasso experts in the world. You've even read that *Garçon avec Cheval* is his favorite painting!

One day you walk into the gallery and see Marsden standing in front of your largest painting. He looks around and recognizes you.

"I can smell the earth and feel the rain," he says, "and the rainbow is more real than any I've seen in the sky!"

You're about to thank him for the compliment when an alarm sounds! You look around the corner to see what's happening. A guard is lying on the floor, rubbing his head. Someone kneels to help him. At that moment you notice a blank space on the wall where the fake Picasso was hung. You run through the lobby and look outside. A blue van races away from the museum and disappears around a corner before you have a chance of spotting its license plate.

Turn to page 19.

"What exactly are you getting at?" Marsden is beginning to look nervous.

"You kept the real one for yourself," you say. "The academy got a fake that you had painted to fool them. Then you arranged for the fake to be stolen. That way, no one could discover the forgery, and the academy would get the insurance money for the missing real Picasso!"

You know by the look on Marsden's face that you've uncovered his scheme. You can't believe he's capable of it, but still . . .

"You're as clever as you are talented," Marsden says, looking too calm. "I'm just sorry you had to figure the whole thing out."

Then you notice the gun in his hand.

If you try to reason with him, turn to page 100.

If you just try to slip out the door, turn to page 102.

You're feeling really good, no doubt about it. On the other hand, it's not all roses. You've been on TV and in the papers so much that everyone recognizes you. You can't walk down the street without a lot of brash people coming up to shake your hand and show you pictures of themselves doing some kind of sport. Some days you sign so many autographs that your hand cramps up.

On the other hand, you do enjoy your sports car, your house on the beach, and being able to help out your family and friends.

Over the next few years you reign supreme in your sport. Sometimes you have a rival—someone who really challenges you. Once in a while you even lose. But most of the time no one can touch you. You've become a legend in your own time.

Eventually you begin to wonder whether you shouldn't be doing something else with your life besides sports. You've certainly had lots of offers. You could go to Hollywood and be a movie actor, or move to Hawaii and just have fun, go into an early retirement. You've even been approached by a group that wants you to run for Congress.

If you go to Hollywood, turn to page 17.

If you go to Hawaii, turn to page 34.

If you decide to run for Congress, turn to page 5.

"You know, Mom, Dad," you say, "I'd really like to try skiing. We're so lucky that Uncle Howard bought that ski lodge in Taos, New Mexico. He said I would be welcome to come visit and learn skiing on my spring vacation."

"Well," your dad says, "that sounds like a great idea."

Uncle Howard sends you a couple of training videos and his own list of ski exercises. "You'll be ahead of the game if you've developed some muscle strength and understand the theory of skiing before you start," he writes.

Uncle Howard gets you on skis almost the moment you arrive in Taos. His daughter (your cousin Tina) is a year younger than you, but she already skis like a demon. You're determined to keep up with her, and then some, by the end of vacation.

Normally, ski teachers start teaching beginners to ski by getting them to use the snowplow turn—where you put your legs out in a V to brake your descent. You try this, but it's boring. You've watched the videos of advanced ski technique so much that you're anxious to ski with your skis parallel, even when you're turning. You try it the first time down the slope, remembering to keep your weight on the downhill ski and to step into your turn, shifting your weight to the ski that's becoming the downhill ski as you turn. It comes to you quickly and easily. You love the feeling! You want to go on steeper slopes and move faster and jump. You're hooked!

Turn to page 86.

When the lights come up, you see that Mr. Raoul and Ms. Winower are smiling.

"You did a great job," says Mr. Raoul. "And don't worry about going over budget. I'm sure we'll make up the difference at the box office."

Mr. Raoul knows what he's talking about. *Final Justice* nets $65,000,000 at the box office in the first year, even before it's released on video. The *Hollywood Reporter* cites you as the best young director of the year.

"You're on your way," says Mr. Raoul. "You're going to be a movie director *superstar!*"

The End

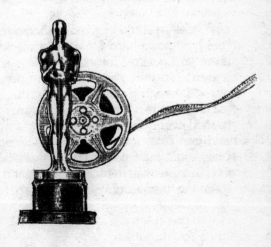

The next days are wild. You'd like to get some rest and spend some time with your family and friends, but calls keep coming in from all over— from people who want to be your agent or manager, from companies wanting you to endorse their product, from publicity agents, politicians, and lecture bureaus—not to mention the fan mail you're getting—about 150 letters a day! You'd have to spend half your time just opening them, much less reading them and writing back.

Fortunately, your friend Maggie has been a big help. She's been opening the mail and making sure you see anything important. One day she waves a letter at you that looks *very* important—it has the great seal of the United States on it. You open it in a hurry.

"It's from the president!" gasps Maggie. "You've been invited to an award banquet!" she continues, reading over your shoulder. You'll be receiving an award for distinguished achievement, along with a famous scientist, an important author, a distinguished artist, and the conductor of the Chicago Symphony Orchestra.

Dinner at the White House is very exciting, although you're seated near the end of the table and don't get much of a chance to talk to the president. You have to sit through a couple of boring speeches, but the food is good, and you enjoy talking to the people next to you.

Turn to page 40.

You duck down as low as you can. Looking up, you see the rifle swinging out, pointing right at you. You try to think of something to say, but you never get the chance.

As you slump to the ground, you hear police sirens. Unfortunately they don't arrive soon enough to save you.

The End

The hard thing is *time*. You want to make music, not just talk, talk, talk. So you tell the group's manager, Gordo Thornton, "I need some peace. I want to write songs. I want to sing and play music."

"That's what I'm here for," Gordo says.

You've heard a lot of stories about bad managers, but Gordo is a good guy, and he knows what he's doing. He deserves as much credit as any of you for your success. By the end of your first year with The Syndrome, you've got three gold albums, two platinum albums, and six Grammy awards.

"You know what that means?" Gordo says. "It means you are a superstar!"

You can't imagine what will happen next, when you get an interesting call from Ken Rascusin. "Guess what?" he says. "We just got a call from Pat Royall, manager for Ginger Blue—he wants to know whether we'd like to have Ginger sing with our group!"

"You're kidding."

"On the level," says Ken.

Turn to page 41.

34

You've got the money so you decide to just have a good time. You buy a nice house on the beach at Maui in Hawaii and start living a life of ease.

Your spread in Maui has four bedrooms and four baths, not counting servants' areas, and a huge deck overlooking the bay, a white sandy beach in front of you, and behind you a tennis court and a pool. If you want to go swimming or windsurfing or play a little tennis you only have to walk a few yards. The coldest it gets here is about sixty degrees, and the sea breeze keeps you from ever getting too hot.

Your fridge is always stocked with cool drinks—your favorite is fresh pineapple juice. There's nothing better since, only minutes before they're made into juice, the pineapples are picked fresh from the plantation next door. Your tremendous assortment of computer games, your huge video library, and your big-screen TV with satellite antenna (you can pick up 139 channels) all keep you pretty well entertained. And of course you have remote control so you never have to get up off the couch to change channels or turn on a good movie.

Turn to page 47.

You have an urge to draw something, so you get a big piece of paper and a pencil and start drawing the first thing that comes into your mind—a Siberian tiger. It's the largest and really most splendid of all tigers, but also very rare. The only Siberian tiger you've ever seen was on television.

Your tiger drawing comes out beautifully, so you decide to do an oil painting. Once you've stretched a huge canvas and primed it, you're ready to paint. You work frantically for hours.

Finally you step back to look at your creation. The tiger is standing majestically in a jungle, wreathed by strange, leafy plants. The tiger peers out at you. He looks tremendously imposing with his splendid mane (something ordinary tigers don't have) and his broad white stripes. Your tiger seems ready to walk out of the jungle and into the room! You can't wait to show your painting to your art teacher, Ms. Tignor.

Turn to page 9.

You call Tim back. "I'd like to join The Syndrome."

"Great," he answers. "We're practicing tonight around six. We really need a keyboard player like you." Tim gives you directions to the rehearsal.

"See you then, Tim." You hang up the phone, do a little dance, and shout. You're going to be a rock star!

Taking a shower before you go out, you're so happy you start singing first a golden oldie, then something just made up on the spot—you call it "Breakdown on the Line."

That night you sing it for The Syndrome.

"That's a great rock-blues number," Tim says.

By the end of the evening, you've shown them how the keyboard should be played, and you've agreed to write three more numbers for the group's upcoming audition with Avanti Records.

Turn to page 50.

"The insurance money?" you ask.

Jason Marsden lowers his eyes. "Yes," he murmurs. "But now I've been caught. I should have known this would happen." He picks up the gun again, but you reach over and gently take it from his hand.

"You don't really want to kill yourself," you say. "You can return the Picasso to the academy. They probably won't even press charges if you tell them your story."

Marsden looks up at you. "I guess I'd rather give up the painting than give up my life."

The End

You let the ball go. "Ball," shouts the ump. The count is 1 and 2.

Dobson, the Twins' pitcher, shakes off a sign, spits, adjusts his cap. He nods at the catcher. He glances back at second, *throws* . . . SMACK! It's a clean hit, through the hole between first and second. You round first. They're going to have to play it off the wall. Koenig scores the tying run as you're on your way to third! You round the bag as the right fielder fires the ball toward the catcher. It'll be close, you realize. You race toward the plate, leaping the last twenty feet, hands outstretched. As you tumble over the plate, you hear the smack of the ball in the catcher's mitt. For a heart-stopping instant, you're not sure if you made it or not. Then you collapse with relief as the ump shouts, "SAFE!"

Go on to the next page.

The crowd goes wild. Your teammates lift you up in the air and carry you off the field. The manager runs up and shakes your hand. About twenty guys with notepads and cameras crowd in behind him.

"So how does it feel to be a superstar?" shouts a reporter, shoving a microphone in your direction.

"It feels great!" You can't stop smiling and laughing. This is a moment you'll never forget. You did it . . . you won the World Series!

Turn to page 27.

After dinner, all eyes are on the president as he stands by the door shaking hands with the departing guests. It's only because of your great peripheral vision that you notice one of the guests slipping a tiny black object behind the gold-leaf frame of a picture of George Washington. You know at once that it must be an electronic "bug." The man who planted it there presses past the others and out the door. You weren't able to get a good look at him.

You hurry outside, hoping to catch sight of him before he disappears, but all you see is the door closing behind a man getting into a black limousine. It pulls down the drive and swings past the gate onto Pennsylvania Avenue. You run after it. The startled marine guard doesn't stop you: his orders are to stop people from getting in, and he has no orders to stop them from leaving, even if they are running.

The limo has already gone a block, but now it's stuck at a light. You race after it, putting on the kind of speed that only a superstar can! The light turns green, but, good luck for you, a bus is blocking the intersection, and the limo is stuck. Suddenly you're alongside the car. You turn to catch a glance inside and are surprised to see that the window is open. You are even more surprised by an automatic rifle pointed dead at you!

If you try to grab the rifle, turn to page 113.

*If you try to duck out of the line of fire,
turn to page 31.*

You can hardly believe your ears. Ginger Blue is the hottest name in pop music. She's been on the scene only three years, and she's already sold eighteen million records. Slinky looking, with long black hair, she's got a voice like a tropical songbird amplified five hundred times. When she sings, she moves and dances and looks at the audience in a way that sends them floating up to the rafters.

"I guess we'll go with that, right, Ken?" you say. "What a combination! Ginger Blue and The Syndrome!"

"Tim doesn't want to take her on," Ken says. "He says she'd eclipse us and we'd lose our identity."

"I guess Tim would lose a little of his," you say. "Nobody else is going to be the lead when Ginger Blue is anywhere near a mike. What about Sally? What does she say?"

"Sally has mixed feelings," Ken says, "and I'm for it and Tim's against it. You're going to have to decide!"

The fact is that you think it would be great to have Ginger Blue in the group. But you can see why Tim doesn't want her. He would take a backseat to her and really wouldn't get much attention. Your first thought is, that's *his* problem, but then you remember that if it hadn't been for Tim you wouldn't be in the group yourself.

*If you vote to take in Ginger Blue,
turn to page 98.*

If you vote to not take her in, turn to page 56.

What else can you say? "We sure will, sir!"

"Many thanks," the president says. "You'll be hearing from my chief of staff."

Click. The line is dead. He doesn't have time to ask about the family and that sort of thing, you think.

In a moment you're back on the phone again, getting hold of the rest of the group.

Six weeks later, your Aeroflot jet sets down in Leningrad. Dawn in Leningrad in May comes at around 2 o'clock in the morning, so you and the rest of the band retire to your hotel where you try to sleep while the sun streams onto your bed through a curtainless window. Around 10 a.m. you're summoned down to the dining room for a breakfast of greasy eggs and black bread you'd need a hacksaw to cut through. Your Russian hosts soon appear. They insist you take a tour through Russia's most famous art museum—the Hermitage. It's full of stunning pictures.

Turn to page 6.

Jenkins doesn't know the half of it. Avanti releases your first singles back-to-back, then comes the album. Alex Bachman, the late-night talk-show sensation, calls *you* to practically beg The Syndrome to appear on his show.

Bachman says he thinks you are the hottest performer of the hottest act in the country!

"It's happening fast," Tim says, and is he ever right. Soon you've got to hire a publicity agent, lawyers, accountants, a booking agent, a secretary, and a manager to manage them all.

Even before you're on the Alex Bachman show, "Breakdown on the Line" hits the *Billboard* charts at number 6 with a bullet. The following week it's first on the charts. Pretty soon you're being interviewed on "Entertainment Tonight" and "Good Morning America," not to mention "The Today Show." It's wild!

Turn to page 32.

Game seven. A pitcher's battle—right up to the last of the ninth, which finds the Cards coming up to bat trailing 2–1. Two out, a runner on second, and you're up! The crowd is going wild. The geatest rookie in the history of the game is at bat. The tying run is on second, winning run at the plate.

The first pitch is a fastball that just catches the strike zone. "Strike one," calls the umpire. You don't care. You didn't like the pitch.

The second pitch looks good, curving. You swing and feel the ball connect with the bat. It's a solid line drive down the left field line! You race toward first. Al Koenig, the runner on second, is already rounding third when the ball curves foul by inches.

Now you're behind 0 and 2 and feeling more nervous than ever—the whole series is hanging on the next pitch. Here it comes. You don't like it, but it could be in the strike zone.

If you decide to swing, turn to page 58.

If you decide to let the ball go by, turn to page 38.

Having decided to be a baseball star, you have to decide what position to play. By the time you've reached high school, your mind is made up—you're going to be a pitcher. Sophomore year you're elected captain of the team. That season you win every game except two, which you would have won if your teammates hadn't made so many errors. Your earned run average for the season is an amazing 1.06.

Junior year things go better. You rack up a 7 and 0 record including two no-hitters. Yet, great as you are at pitching, you begin to wonder about playing another position. Your hitting is good. You batted .420 as a pitcher your junior year, and though you're not exactly a power hitter, you're so fast that more often than not you stretch singles into doubles and triples, not to mention two inside-the-park home runs.

You're especially lucky that the team coach, Hal Walters, has one of the smartest baseball minds around. He played one fantastic year with the Yankees and was almost elected rookie of the year. Then a car crash shattered his arm and ended his career. When he knew he'd never play pro ball again, Hal went into teaching, coaching baseball on the side.

Turn to page 57.

One day your neighbor, Ken Sato, pays a call on you. He's usually a happy, smiling man but today he looks tense.

"I got troubles," he says. "My pineapple plants are dying as soon as they sprout. At the rate things are going, I won't have any crop at all, and I'll be wiped out. I'll have to sell my place for a song."

You're sad to hear this because you know that Ken was born on his pineapple plantation and it means a great deal to him. Besides that, if the plantation goes, you won't get super fresh juice anymore!

"Maybe some bugs are getting them," you say.

Ken shakes his head. "Nope, we've tested for everything, and it's just as much a mystery as ever."

"Could someone have put something toxic in the soil?"

Ken runs his fingers through his thin black hair. "No—we tested for that too. I'm replanting tomorrow—it's the only thing I can do."

"Well, I hope your luck changes," you say.

Go on to the next page.

After Ken leaves, you read about Jack Sarino, a developer who is trying to buy up land cheap in the area. The article says he's one of the slickest operators on the island. Could there be some connection between Jack Sarino and Ken's pineapple problem? you wonder.

The next day you stake out and watch Ken planting. You keep an eye on his field each day from then on. You're feeling really happy when you see the first little pineapple sprouts have come up. They look as green and healthy as could be. They're getting plenty of sun and water. They should grow fast. You decide to check them again first thing tomorrow morning.

Turn to page 60.

Six weeks later you are at the Avanti recording studios in Alameda. Chick Graybar, the chief producer of Avanti, and Jason Jenkins, the company president, are both there. They were so taken with the demo they got from The Syndrome that they came down to the studio to see what your group could do. Well, they aren't disappointed, because you and Tim, with Sally Kalchek on drums, and Ken Rascusin on second guitar, let loose with some of the wildest music you've ever heard, much less played. Chick and Jason go bananas. They're on the phone halfway through, calling in their marketing and promo people, and before you've walked out of the studio you've not only shaken hands on a three-year recording deal, but they've mapped out a twelve-state tour followed by appearances in Tokyo, Hong Kong, Melbourne, Rio, and Mexico City.

Turn to page 44.

When you finally get a feeble return over the net, Blair puts it away with such force that the ball bounces up into the stands. Then Blair breaks you again. You win the next two points, but Blair, still in command, keeps you on the defensive the next game and wins it with a neat half volley.

Each of you wins your next two serves. Now it's your serve at 5–6. You concentrate, you serve well each point, but Blair keeps hitting it back. The game goes to deuce three times; then you have to fight off a match point! After that you bear down with a pair of great serves and win the game, forcing Blair into the tiebreaker.

Blair serves the first point in the tiebreaker. You try to keep an eye on it as it hits the tape right at the corner, as pretty an ace as you've ever seen. It's your serve now—you've got to reach a higher level of tennis. You think back to what Steve told you.

Your racket comes down on the ball—a terrific smash, and you put away Blair's weak return. Blair wins two of the next three points and he leads 3–2.

Turn to page 20.

52

You decide to think for a while before you make any decisions about your future. But you've got too much energy to just do nothing. Your school has a creative arts program, and every student gets a chance at using the video camera to make a 12-minute film. You spend a lot of time on yours. Though the film only runs 12 minutes, you spend months making it. Your movie is titled *Final Justice*. It's about a kid named Franz who is a little out of it. The other kids make fun of him, but eventually Franz outsmarts them all.

You decide to send the film off to the president of Continental Film Group, the movie company that made your favorite movie of the past year— *Crash!*

You spend the next few months in a state of suspense waiting to hear from Continental Film Group—until one night when you're woken from a sound sleep. It must be almost midnight when the phone rings. You pick it up and listen to the sweetest words you've ever heard.

Turn to page 85.

From then on you ski every chance you can get. You're not as lucky as kids who live near a major ski area, but you can still get to ski on all your vacations and weekends. And, while you're in high school, you go back to Taos every spring vacation to work with Franz Weber. Then, your senior year, you earn a berth on the Olympic training team where you find yourself competing against kids who have practically lived on skis since they were five years old! Thanks to your fantastic ability, and those years of training under the great Franz Weber, you can compete with the best of them.

Turn to page 90.

You cover the rough ground with the speed of an Olympic hurdler and reach the truck a few yards ahead of the man. You dive through the open window of the truck and land on a shotgun! You're about to grab the gun when you hear a surly voice behind you.

"Get out of there," says the man. "And don't try anything." He yanks open the door. With lightning speed, you kick both your legs into his chest. As he stumbles, you grab the shotgun. He tries to regain his footing, but you knock his gun out of his hand and shove him to the ground.

Now you've got the shotgun trained on him.

"Don't shoot," he begs. His voice is full of panic. You grab the bag he's holding and spill out the contents. At your feet lies a pile of little white chips, each of them smoking as if about to burst into flames. They are bits of dry ice! He was freezing those new plants—and by morning the evidence would have melted!

"You're Jack Sarino, aren't you?" you ask.

He bites his lip, refusing to look at you. "I guess you got me."

You march Sarino down to Ken Sato's farmhouse and call the police.

A few weeks later Ken Sato's new pineapple crop is doing just fine. As for Jack Sarino, he'll be in jail for a long time. And as for you . . . well, Ken Sato has promised you a lifetime supply of the best pineapple juice in the world—a drink fit for a superstar!

The End

You just don't want to let Tim down; besides, there's something to what he says. The Syndrome should try to be great on its own and not change its personality in order to merge with Ginger Blue.

During the months ahead you have good reason to be happy about your decision because The Syndrome takes off more than ever. Your albums are the best selling in the industry, and you do more and more singing. Your rendition of your new song, "Cave Boy Boogie," has all the deejays sitting up and blinking their eyes. The gold records and platinum records and Grammys pile up. You stack them all on a closet shelf because you don't want to clutter up the place.

By this time you've got a house in Malibu, a condo on Maui, a studio overlooking Central Park in New York, and a little red Fiat Spider convertible. Even so, you're not really one of the big spenders. In fact you've been giving at least half your income to charity and another hunk to your folks back home.

Maybe it's because of your association with good causes as much as because you're the biggest superstar of the decade, bigger even, it turns out, than Ginger Blue, that you get a call from the President of the United States one night as you're ready to slip into the Jacuzzi.

"Mr. President," you say into the phone, respectfully. "Hi."

Turn to page 7.

Before the senior year season begins, you decide to talk to Hal about switching positions.

Hal hesitates for a moment before he answers you. "Having you on the team," he says, "we'll be State champions for sure, if you keep pitching. If you switched to another position, we probably wouldn't do as well. Even if you batted a thousand, that wouldn't save us if our pitching was no good. Nobody can pitch half as well as you can."

"Well," you say, "I guess that settles it—I'll keep pitching."

But Hal shakes his head. "Look, kid, I've got more to think about than putting together a string of victories. I'm interested in seeing you develop your skills and sportsmanship as much as possible. That's a lot more important than how many games we win or lose."

"So what should I do?" you ask. Hal rubs his chin and thinks.

Turn to page 65.

You decide to go for it. You swing with everything you've got. *Home run* is the only thing in your mind. Are you ever surprised when you hear the umpire shout, "Strike three! You're out!"

For a moment you're paralyzed. You hear the crowd going crazy, but you also hear them

booing—and they're booing you. You've just lost the World Series single-handedly.

Well, even superstars mess up sometimes.

The End

When you arrive the next day at dawn, you see that several new rows of plants have sprouted. They look perfectly healthy. However, the plants that sprouted yesterday have turned brown and withered, as if they hadn't gotten any rain in a couple of weeks. You bend over, searching for signs of pests or chemicals, but there's nothing. You do notice something—a footprint. Someone has been here. But why?

You decide to return to the field later that night. You hide in the brush at the edge of the field. After hours of waiting, you finally see something. A pickup truck with its lights off pulls toward the field. A minute later a man carrying a large sack gets out of the truck and begins walking through the pineapple sprouts. It's dark, but in the moonlight you can just make out that the man is pulling something from the sack. He stops often, you figure by each sprout.

You decide to check out the truck, but before you reach it you step on a fallen branch. The man stops. You freeze, but he must have seen you, because a moment later you hear a gunshot. It misses you. You race toward the truck with the stranger in hot pursuit, shooting after you. It's a good thing you're a superstar.

Turn to page 54.

Your career as a center fielder proceeds just as Hal had predicted. You lead the team to the longest string of victories in its history. By the time you're ready to graduate from high school, you've already gotten some tempting offers from major league clubs. It happens that you end up with the St. Louis Cardinals. The manager—Ted Nystrom—thinks you're so good that he arranges for you to start in the middle of the season.

Only a week after graduation your dream comes true. You put on a major league uniform. What a thrill it is—standing out in center field, listening to the playing of the national anthem—and then the roar of the crowd as the umpire yells, "Play ball!"

You're a little shaky at first, going only one for four and misjudging a fly ball—catching it only at the last second after making a desperate lunge.

The next day you get two hits, and from then on you begin to sizzle. The Cards do well too, and by the end of the season your team has clinched the pennant and you're a sure shot for rookie of the year. Your batting average is national news—.413. It won't go in the record book because you only played half the season, but there's always next year!

Turn to page 66.

Each contestant has three jumps. The longest jump you can make is the one that counts. The morning dawns gray and drizzly. It doesn't bode well for setting the record. The running ramp may be slippery and soft, making it hard to reach top speed.

Great as you are, you do have a challenger: Andras Zigsgreb of Yugoslavia. Andras holds the world record. Sportscasters call him the Kangaroo. In a publicity stunt in Melbourne, he actually outjumped three kangaroos.

Out on the field you limber up. The truth is, you're worried. For some reason you're not feeling too well, and your first two jumps fall well short of your expectations. They are great by ordinary standards, enough to assure you a silver medal, but a silver medal is not what you're looking for.

Andras, on the other hand, is red-hot. His first two jumps clear 9 meters, and his final jump carries him 9.4 meters—a new world record!

You know you can jump that far, but for the first time in your career you're feeling shaky. It's like a ray of sunshine when you see Bob Waskowitz walking toward you. You haven't seen him in a while, since you stopped competing in high school events, but he's still the best coach you've ever had.

Turn to page 80.

You get a great feeling of accomplishment from making the movie and working with a great director like Sheldon Carver. And it's nice to know that audiences all over the world will be seeing the film.

When the filming is over, you're almost sorry to say good-bye. "You've done a great job," Sheldon says. "I think our film is a good bet to get an Academy Award. And I think *you* have what it takes to be a movie star!" Sheldon shakes your hand as he keeps on talking. "I'd like to have you in my next film. It's going to be about a famous painter who gets lost in the jungles of the Amazon."

"Thanks very much, Sheldon, but I think I'll skip it this time."

Turn to page 72.

"You have a terrific eye—the best I've ever seen in baseball—and a good clean swing," Hal says. "I know that even if you had only average speed you could hit .350 by the time you reach the majors—and I'm sure you *will* reach the majors—but your speed is much better than average. I hear you were clocked at 9.7 in the 100-yard dash—and you hadn't even trained for the event! When I think how many bunts you could beat out, how many bases you could steal, and how many singles you could stretch into extra base hits . . . why, the thought of it dazzles me!"

"I see what you mean, coach. What position do you have in mind?"

"Center field," Hal says without hesitation. "You're so fast you could cover half the outfield. The left and right fielders would be able to cover the foul lines that way. And with your great arm you could get the ball back to the infield fast."

Hal seems real sure of himself, and you like what he says, but you're a little reluctant to give up pitching. "I've improved a lot in pitching," you say. "It's kind of a big jump to switch to center field."

"You've heard of Babe Ruth?" Hal asks with a smile.

"Sure, of course," you say.

"Well, he started out as a pitcher, and he probably would have racked up a pretty good record if he'd stayed at it."

"I get the idea. I'll give center field a try."

Turn to page 61.

Next year, as the World Series begins, the St. Louis Cardinals versus the Minnesota Twins, you're really under pressure. The Twins have a terrific team this year. A lot of the sportscasters are saying they'd be favored to win the series "if it weren't for the Cards' sensational new rookie." They mean *you*, of course. It's as if everyone on and off the team expects *you* to win the series almost single-handedly.

It's opening day of the series, and you're feeling more nervous than you did on your first day playing major league ball. You can't stop thinking about how much depends on your performance.

The first day you go 0 for 4, and your fielding is nothing special. What's worse, the one time you get on base—on a walk in the seventh—you're picked off. The Cards lose 6 to 3.

The next five games go better. The Cards win three of them, evening the series at 3–3. You bring your series batting average up to .327, but you're still not playing the kind of spectacular ball that won your club the pennant.

Turn to page 45.

Finally you sign up for the film, pending one condition—you'll be doing all the skating. You realize your fans would be totally disappointed if you let someone else be the star athlete in the film. It would really be phony. You also know you're a much better athlete than you are an actor.

After a lot of haggling, Sheldon agrees to go along with you on this point. Besides, what appeals to you most about the project is the fact that you'll face a real challenge in learning to be an expert figure skater in only a few short months.

Turn to page 76.

You consider trying to talk these goons out of beating you up, but when you see how they're smiling at each other, you realize nothing you say will change their minds. You're about to steel yourself for the first punch when you look up and see a way out.

Above your head is a fire escape. It's a jump most people couldn't make—but you're not like most people!

You step back a few paces. The goons move toward you, fists clenched, but you hardly seem to notice. Mory, Deke, and Sid are surprised at how calm you appear as they close in.

Suddenly you leap! Your fingers wrap around the bottom rung of the ladder. Like an expert gymnast, you pull yourself up and flip onto the bars of the fire escape so that you're hanging by your knees.

You're congratulating yourself on your clever escape, racing past the first landing of the fire escape, when you knock into a flowerpot.

Turn to page 75.

When Mory Layton finally shows up at school a couple of days later with a big bandage over one eye, he doesn't say a word to you. You're pretty sure he won't be causing you any more trouble.

In the meantime, you've returned to the alley to measure the distance of the jump you made. You can hardly believe your eyes. The tape measure reads 14 feet. Since your reach is only about 7 feet, it means that your feet must have been 7 feet off the ground—pretty close to the world record high jump. Of course, if you were high jumping, you'd have to get even higher off the ground to be sure your body would clear the horizontal bar.

Still, it's a pretty impressive height, and you decide to talk with Bob Waskowitz, your coach, about adding the high jump to the list of track events you're going out for. It's an important decision, because it's only a year and a half until the next Olympics, and you want to be in them!

Turn to page 78.

"It might be a little harder with a football uniform on, carrying a ball and dodging tacklers," you say, smiling.

"Well, maybe a little harder." Turning serious, Bob says, "Of course you'll never have to try a stunt like that—you're going to *specialize* in the long jump. Specialization is the key—that and concentration."

"Thirty feet . . . OK, coach. I'll go for it!"

The next year is tremendously exciting. You break one record after another in school, regional, and national competition. Meanwhile your training continues.

"Ninety per cent of the long jump is speed—because the moment you leave the ground, you're falling," your coach tells you. "Whether you're traveling twenty miles an hour or two miles an hour, gravity starts pulling you down the moment your feet leave the ground. You've got to cover as much distance as possible before you hit. The only way to do that is to be as fast as possible."

"But isn't it important for me to jump as high as I can, too?" you ask. "Then I'll have more time before I hit the ground."

"That's true," says Waskowitz, "but up is not where you want to go. *Ahead* is where you want to go. Sure, you have to get high enough to be off the ground—and you sacrifice a little speed for that—but you can't give up much speed, or you'll never land where you want."

Turn to page 79.

"I'm very disappointed to hear that," Sheldon says. "Tell me, what do you plan to do now?"

"Can't you guess?" you say. "Figure skating! I've gotten to like that better than anything. It's like a sport and dancing at the same time. What could be better than that?"

Sheldon smiles and drapes his big arm around your shoulder. "Well, I'll miss you, kid, but I'm not going to try to talk you out of it. I think you've got what it takes to be a great figure skater. In fact, I think you're going to be a superstar all over again!"

The End

"But how do I do it?" you say, knowing Bob is right.

"Forget about the Olympics. Tell me this: do you like to jump?"

"You bet I do."

Bob stops, and you turn to look at him. "What is it you like about jumping?" he asks.

You break into a grin, thinking about the answer. "I like the way I start—building up speed, and then letting myself go, so I'm not thinking, my body is in control, and . . . I feel like a cheetah—giving everything over to *speed*. Then, at the moment my toe last touches the ground and I'm going so fast I could be flying, I'm running on air!"

"Fantastic!" Bob is beaming. "Now you're in a good mental state. You don't need to worry about the Olympics. All you need to do is let yourself go—and *jump!*"

Turn to page 88.

Unfortunately, some of the other kids are jealous of how good you are. Mory Layton, who is right guard on the football team, is one of them, and so are a couple of buddies of his: Deke Crowley and Sid Olson.

One afternoon on your way home from school you're cutting through a narrow alley when you see Mory coming at you from ahead. He stops, arms crossed, glaring at you. You know you're in for trouble.

"What do you want?" you ask.

A kind of sly grin spreads across his face. "You've been moving a little too fast," he says. "I'm going to slow you up a little."

At first, you're not particularly worried. You know you can run at least three times as fast as Mory, but when you turn around, you see Deke and Sid coming right at you! They aren't that much bigger than you, but now they've got you surrounded.

Turn to page 68.

You turn around in time to see the pot falling—straight onto Mory's head.

Mory lies moaning in the alley. He has a cut over his eye, but you can tell by all his weeping and wailing that his thick head saved him from serious injury.

The other two guys are standing there looking stupid as the lady who owns the flowerpot comes out of her apartment onto the fire escape, shaking her finger at you.

"What's going on here?" she demands suspiciously. You try to explain, but she doesn't believe your story. Neither do the police who arrive moments later.

"Maybe a kangaroo could make a jump like that, kid," says one cop, "but you couldn't."

There's only one way to prove that you're telling the truth. You make the jump again. That satisfies the police and the lady. They tell you to stay out of trouble. Then they help Mory to a squad car and drive him home.

Turn to page 70.

After four months of intensive training, you're satisfied that you are skating well enough to go in front of the cameras. Filming takes place in Montreal where there is good skating indoors and out. The movie is fun to make, though it's a lot harder work than you'd expected. Every time you get tired of a scene, Sheldon decides he's not satisfied and insists on shooting it over and over, trying different camera angles, changing the lights. Like all great directors, he's a perfectionist.

Still, you're having a great time. Your skating is getting better every day, and your fans love you more than ever for undertaking such a tough project. Even when it's freezing outside, there's always a crowd of fans waiting to watch the filming, crowding behind police barricades to get a glimpse of you in action.

One day Sheldon pulls you aside.

"I can hardly believe it—but you really have become an incredible skater," Sheldon says. He's so impressed with your new skills that he calls in the writers to change the script. "We're going to put a lot more emphasis on the skating to really highlight your ability," he says.

Turn to page 64.

Bob won a bronze medal in the 100-meter dash eleven years ago, and you're anxious to know what he thinks your chances might be in a number of events. When you tell him, Bob seems impressed with the distance you jumped.

"You might pick up a medal in five or six events," he says, "including the high jump. I'm pretty sure you could pick up a gold medal in any distance under eight hundred meters. In fact, I think you could someday break the world record in the hundred-meter dash and the two hundred-meter dash, but there's one event where you could do even better than that."

"Better than that? Gosh, coach, what are you talking about?"

"What I'm talking about is the long jump. I think you could be the first human to jump more than ten meters—that's thirty-two feet, seven inches."

"Thirty-two feet?" You repeat the words, trying to visualize the distance.

"In football, that means you could receive the ball, first and ten, take off at the line of scrimmage, and when your feet hit the turf you'd have made a first down."

"Sounds out of this world!"

"No use throwing the ball ten yards when you can throw *yourself* that far." Waskowitz laughs with delight.

"Ten meters—thirty-two feet. What's the world record now, coach?" you wonder.

"Twenty-nine feet, three inches."

Turn to page 71.

You learn a lot more in your training. You discover that *concentrating* is letting the body take over the mind, rather than trying to analyze every motion you make.

Training and concentration, these things, coupled with your fantastic talent, are what take you to the top.

By the time the Olympics come, you're famous. Every sportscaster has interviewed you or tried to interview you. You've been on the cover of half a dozen magazines. You've *already* broken the world record (unofficially) in the long jump. You're the favorite to win the gold medal—and you're still a teenager.

MILAN, ITALY—SITE OF YOUR FIRST OLYMPICS

Everything has been a preparation for this. The whole world is watching, and not just because this is the most important sporting event in the world—held only once every four years—but because people expect something very special from you.

By the final day of competition you've won the gold medal in the 100-meter dash and in the 200-meter dash. You're happy with your wins, but now it is time for the long jump. You know you're good, probably a shoo-in for the gold, but you're still nervous. Will you be the first human to do 10 meters in the long jump?

Turn to page 63.

"I had some trouble getting onto the field," he calls to you. "They wouldn't believe I was your high school coach until I showed them your autographed picture inscribed to me."

Smiling, you slap a hand on Bob's shoulder. "I wouldn't even be here if it weren't for you."

"I watched your first two jumps," he says. "You looked a little unsure of yourself."

"I seem to be getting tired of it all, the pressure—the fact that everyone's watching—that I *have* to perform. Much as I want to win, something's holding me back. I can't explain it."

Bob shakes his head.

"Look," he says. "You've got ten minutes before it's time for your third jump. Let's take a walk."

"Sure."

As the two of you stroll along the track, ignoring the pole-vaulting competition taking place only a couple of dozen yards away, Bob speaks his mind.

"What you're going through has happened to others a thousand times before. You have to remember you're not a running and jumping machine—you're a human being. The trouble is that you've slipped into a bad mental state; you've psyched yourself out. Now what you need to do is get back to feeling really good about jumping."

Turn to page 73.

Zrigrn is like a meteor. You watch the run on the monitor, listening to the whoops of the crowd along the trail. Elsin's skis are clattering on the bumps, his hand is only inches above the snow on the turns. His time at the gates ticks off as he goes racing through the finish in 1.57.06 seconds. *Unbelievable!*

You sort of space out as the next few skiers take their runs. None of them is going to threaten Zrigrn. You race the course in your mind, concentrating, visualizing the turns, the jumps—there won't be time to think on the way down.

Go on to the next page.

At last your moment arrives. With a terrific thrust, you're off—hurtling down the mountain, flying, keeping your speed in the turns, picking up speed on the bumps, gliding, jumping, tucking in. You make a tremendous leap off a bump and your leg almost goes out, but you don't slow down. You keep driving hard, hard, hard.

You fly around the last turn!

Go on to the next page.

Suddenly, ahead, you see a sheer drop with only a scattering of rocky-looking moguls to brake your speed. The snow has iced up since Elsin raced. You see glassy patches everywhere as you crouch low, gathering speed.

You've raced well, but your time so far can't be as good as Elsin's. You're going to have to give it something extra. You're going to have to take the moguls in jumps, or schuss it down the bare, icy slope!

*If you schuss it down the icy slope,
turn to page 18.*

*If you take on the moguls and try to pick up
speed in the jumps, turn to page 112.*

"You're the creator of *Final Justice?*" the voice on the phone demands.

"I sure am," you say sleepily.

"Well this is Norman Raoul, of Continental Film Group—and we think this is the most brilliant screenplay that's come in here in a long time."

"Gosh, thank you, Mr. Raoul."

"It's not long enough or technically adequate to be released as a feature film, of course, but we want you to come out to Hollywood and we'll work with you. If you're interested, give me a call within the next couple of days, but no more than that. We're pretty active here, and I can't promise you I won't be shooting a film in Australia or Africa next week."

"Sure, thank you—I'll get back to you tomorrow."

Click. The phone goes dead. Mr. Raoul is obviously one of these high-pressure movie moguls who's all business and no small talk. He must be a brilliant producer, but he doesn't sound as if he's the sort you could get to know very well.

In the morning you discuss Raoul's offer with your parents.

"It sounds like a wonderful opportunity," your father says, "but it doesn't seem right to drop out of school."

"I could go to school out there," you say.

Turn to page 97.

You take a few spills but you learn from them, and thanks to your exercises, your muscles aren't even sore at the end of the day. After a week you have no trouble beating Tina down the mountain. You're even able to give Uncle Howard a good race.

The second week of your vacation you train with Franz Weber, the top instructor. A few days with Franz and you're racing down Whirlaway, Kingman's Chute, and the other super-steep runs. Franz straightens out the kinks in your form, and he helps you get the right mental attitude so that you're skiing in a smooth, flowing motion. Then he clocks you down the racecourse. That night he comes over to have dinner with you and Uncle Howard at the lodge.

Franz is all smiles, and he comes straight to the point. "In the sixteen years I've been an instructor, including coaching two Olympic teams, I've never seen such a natural skier as you. It's as if you were born on skis! Born to conquer mountains! I see the Olympics in your future."

"Gosh, which event?" you ask, blushing at Franz's praise.

"All the basic events—slalom, giant slalom, super giant slalom and downhill. Especially downhill. That to me is the one that means the most."

You hardly know what to say—you're awed.

"Of course," Uncle Howard says, "you've got a long way to go."

Turn to page 53.

Suddenly everything goes black. When you regain consciousness a few minutes later, you realize you've broken your leg, badly. It takes a little longer to realize that despite everything, you've won the silver medal.

Someone is grabbing your hand—it's Elsin Zrigrn!

"I wouldn't have made the time you did over those moguls," he says. "You're a superstar, kid."

As you're taken away on a stretcher, you hold onto those words, hoping you'll have another chance to race Elsin—and win the gold!

The End

88

You hardly have time to thank Bob, because it's suddenly time for your event. You feel as if a burden has been lifted from your shoulders, and from your legs! You feel light and happy, and more than anything in the world, you want to *jump!*

You race down the track, gathering speed, then spring up—*racing* on air. When your feet touch down, you know you've won *everything:* the gold, the world record, and the 10-meter barrier!

As the results are announced, first in Italian and then in English, a great rolling cheer fills the stadium. People are rushing toward you from all directions. Microphones, cameras are everywhere. It's at that moment, for the first time really, that you know you're a superstar!

Turn to page 30.

90

At last the moment has come. This year the winter Olympics are being held in Squaw Valley, California. You have performed sensationally up until now, and you're the main hope of the U.S. Olympic team, but you're up against terrific competition. Elsin Zrigrn of Switzerland is probably the toughest. Elsin holds more downhill titles than anyone in the history of the sport. Here is the skier with legs of steel. You believe it, having seen him streaking down a cliff, skis clattering on the ice, always pointed downward, never letting up the pace.

They've called you a superstar, the best American downhill skier ever, but it's Elsin Zrigrn who's favored to win the Olympics.

The day you'll face Elsin comes, and it's bitter cold and a gusty wind is blowing snow off the peaks. There's talk of a postponement, but word comes that the race will be held. You've drawn twelfth position in the lottery, and Elsin has drawn third. That's not good news for you. The track deteriorates a little after each run, so you'll be at a disadvantage, but no matter. You're not going to start thinking of excuses.

Turn to page 94.

When you get out to Hollywood, you find that Mr. Raoul is out of town.

"He's gone to India to deal with a problem we have on a movie in production there," his assistant, Ms. Luchek, tells you.

Good grief, you think, your mom was right! You're ready to turn around and go home, but Ms. Luchek says she wants you to see Sandy Winower, another producer.

"Don't worry," says Winower, "I've cleared the decks to work with you on *Final Justice.*"

From then on your life is busy. When you're not at the computer working over the screenplay for *Final Justice,* you're busy working out technical problems, or auditioning actors. Things move along quickly though, and by the time Mr. Raoul gets back from India, you're ready to start production.

It's grueling work, making a film—you often have to shoot a scene several times over until it seems just right. The scenes aren't always shot in the order they'll appear in the film, so it can get confusing too. You've also got to be careful to stay within a pretty tight budget. Every night the accountants remind you that the whole film is going to be scrapped if you can't cut costs. At the same time Mr. Raoul is telling you that if you aren't a perfectionist you might as well go home.

The last scene of *Final Justice* is shot two weeks after your deadline. Production costs are ten percent over budget.

Turn to page 95.

You throw the ball high, pointing toward it as it falls. SMASH. An ace!

You serve again, a good hard one, but Tony returns it deep on your backhand side. You reach it and send it crosscourt. Tony hits it back. You stroke it down the line and run for the net, ready to put it away if it comes back, but Tony somehow gets to it and sends a beautiful lob over your head toward the far corner. You race for it, stretching as the ball bounces off the baseline, and whip a strong forehand across the court! Tony leaps for it. The ball drops on your side of the net at the other side of the court. It's an impossible attempt, but you go for it. You dive, slam the ball, and flip it over Tony's head. You make the point!

Go on to the next page.

From then on you're playing tennis the way it should be played—and you completely forget about Steve Chandler up in the stands. You go on to beat the number one player in straight sets!

It's not until that evening at dinner that you see Steve Chandler again. He comes up to you as you're leaving for the movies with some of your friends.

"I watched you play today," he says.

"Oh, thanks. It was a good match for me," you say.

"Indeed it was," Steve says. "Be at the courts at nine tomorrow. I want you to play an exhibition match."

Turn to page 104.

Suddenly it's all happening! Milo Cavender of Canada is racing down the slope, disappearing in a cloud of blowing snow. Milo's time is relayed from the bottom—2.01.88 seconds. A very strong performance. Cavender may pick up the bronze.

Then Hals Verstmann of Austria—still with two steel pins in each knee from a bad spill at Zermatt last year. He's good, but you're not worried about him.

Then Elsin Zrigrn, orange gloves flashing, pushes out of the starter gate and thrusts to full speed, hurtling down the mountain.

Turn to page 81.

Now you've got to take the film to be edited. Many sleepless nights later you have a finished movie. You invite Ms. Winower and Mr. Raoul to a private screening. You're really nervous, sitting in the dark waiting for the film to roll. If they don't like the movie, your career as a director is over. And since you went over budget and past your deadline shooting and editing, they're expecting great things.

Still, as you watch the film you have to admit that it's good. By the time the credits flash on the screen, you're feeling pretty confident.

Turn to page 29.

You've gotten to know where the ball is going just by seeing the way your opponent is approaching it. Sometimes you get fooled, but even then you're terrific at changing direction and retrieving a ball that looked like a winner.

One day you start out playing pretty well in a three-set match against Tony Stanberg, who is first on the tennis ladder. Tony is very strong and has been playing a serve and volley game against you. Usually this spells defeat for his opponent, but you've been practicing your passing shots. More than once you leave Tony standing helplessly at the net while your ball rifles down the line. That's what happens when you win the tiebreaker of the first set. Suddenly you feel nervous—you have a chance to beat the number one player in the best tennis camp in the country!

As you're changing sides after the first set, Tony motions toward the stands. "Look who's sitting in the top row."

You glance up there—it's Steve Chandler himself. Now you feel really nervous.

It's your serve. You double-fault twice and miss a half volley with no power in it. You could have won the point easily; instead you hit the ball too hard, and Tony puts it away. Love–40.

You wonder if Steve is still watching. Probably he's gotten bored and gone home. You don't dare look up to see. If a player is self-conscious, it means he or she is not concentrating on the game. You've heard Steve say that himself. And one thing you've got to do now is concentrate!

Turn to page 92.

"Maybe you could take classes out there," says your mom, "and maybe you wouldn't have time. Some of these show biz types talk fast but then they don't necessarily follow up on their promises. You could get out there and find that Mr. Raoul is off on some other project. The whole deal could fall through, and Mr. Raoul might just say, 'Sorry, kid, never mind.'"

You spend the rest of the day trying to make a decision. Finally you call Mr. Raoul and tell him you're on your way to Hollywood. After all, if things don't work out, you can always come back home and continue with school.

Turn to page 91.

You were afraid that Tim would take it pretty hard when you voted to let Ginger Blue in the band, but he's a great guy and he says, "I'll make out all right."

Ginger turns out to be a terrific addition. She inspires you to write some great new songs. One of them, "Moonbaby," performed by Ginger Blue and The Syndrome, achieves the greatest sale of any single in history. The flip side—you and Ginger doing a duet of another one of your songs, "Racing on the River"—ends up getting almost as

much airplay as "Moonbaby"! *Time* magazine ends up putting Ginger on the cover—as Woman of the Year. Things work out better than any of you expected with Tim and Ginger. Ginger's voice is such an inspiration that Tim can't help but write a string of super hits for her and even a couple of duets for the two of them.

Turn to page 11.

"Don't do anything you'd be sorry for," you say. Marsden's fingers close on the gun. You hear him release the safety catch. "You'll never get away with it," you say in an even tone. "Too many people know I'm here."

The director's face is as pale as skim milk, his eyes glazed. "I wasn't thinking of shooting you," he says, his voice cracking. "I was planning to shoot myself."

"Why don't you turn yourself in to the police instead?" you say.

Marsden heaves a tremendous sigh. "I never meant for it to happen this way. When the academy bought the painting I became obsessed. I *had* to have the Picasso for myself. But I'm not a thief by nature, so I tried to think of a way to make up the money to the museum."

Turn to page 37.

Two years have passed. You're out of college and playing on the pro circuit, moving up in the rankings, when you win the Australian Open. Sportscasters all over the world are calling you the one to watch. GREATEST SINCE BORG? says a headline in the *Times*.

Maybe the headline should have read FLASH IN THE PAN? In the Italian Open you're beaten in the second round by a player who wasn't even seeded for the tournament. You're feeling pretty discouraged when you get a call from your old friend, Steve Chandler.

"Look, you're not a machine, you're a human," he tells you. "Everybody has a bad match now and then. The main thing is not to let it get you down, but to see it as part of the rhythm of things. Before you start training for the French Open, take a few days off, get together with some friends, have fun. To win in tennis you have to enjoy life, otherwise you'll turn into a tennis machine. You may win a few tournaments, but you'll never be great unless you love to play."

Turn to page 109.

You start to back out the door. In a single motion Marsden releases the safety and trains the gun at your chest. You duck. A shot rings out. But no bullet has struck you. You start to run, but glancing back, you see Marsden slumped over his desk. You look at him more closely and at the bullet hole in his suit. Marsden is dead!

You don't know whether to feel sorry for Marsden or relieved that he didn't shoot you. You don't have long to think about it anyway, because soon his office is swarming with guards and police. You tell them everything you know.

When you finally leave, you're tired and depressed. You keep wondering if you could have stopped Marsden.

Maybe painting will make you feel better, you think. Then again, maybe not.

The End

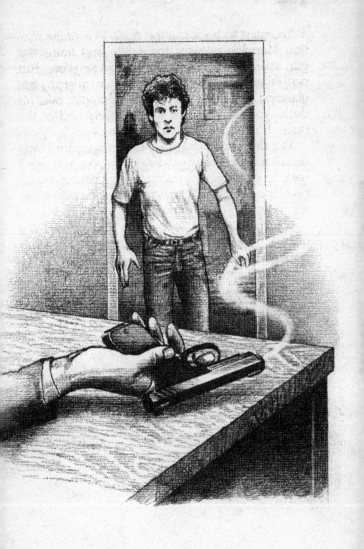

You're so excited about playing an exhibition match that you arrive early. You are surprised to see your opponent already there, warming up with Steve. You can hardly believe it. Steve has arranged for you to play against Rene Levaque, the sixth-ranked player in the *world*.

Early in the match the two of you have some long volleys that you think will never end. You each win a set. By the third set you're beginning to feel a little tired. More and more Rene presses close to the net, driving you back to the corners. You're a little discouraged when you lose the set 7–5 and the match 6–3, 5–7, 7–5. But then everyone flocks around you! Only then do you remember that you played the sixth-ranked player in the world and almost won!

When you leave camp and head back to school, you're sure you made the right decision. Tennis is your game.

Turn to page 101.

Blair was seeded number one and you number two in the tournament. No one is surprised that the two of you are paired off in the finals. It's being called the match of the decade. You're both in top form, and the fans can hardly contain their excitement. A lot of them are rooting for you because you're the rising star and because people like you, but a lot of fans are rooting for Blair Caukins. After all, he is a tennis legend.

The weather is hot and muggy. The two of you battle it out. It seems as if the match will go on forever as you and Blair stand even, going into the deciding set.

You get off to a good start, breaking Blair's first service, but then your serve falters, and Blair breaks back. During the next game you struggle desperately, returning well, but the ball keeps booming back at you.

Turn to page 51.

Suddenly a siren blares, and a searchlight blinds you.

"Drop it!" You hear a policeman's voice over a loudspeaker.

You drop the gun.

Horns blare. Traffic is stopped in all directions. Two unmarked cars screech to a halt. Plainclothes agents leap out, guns drawn, not on you—on the limo!

"FBI," one of the agents shouts.

Suddenly there are agents and cops all over the place.

Slowly the limo doors open. Three men get out—one by one—hands in the air. One of them is the man you saw plant the bug in the White House.

An FBI man taps your shoulder.

"Thanks for your help, superstar," he says.

The End

"The Syndrome has done a wonderful job," he says. "Thanks to the success of your visit we plan to begin a major cultural exchange between our countries. You have made history here!"

"Wahoo!" you shout after you've hung up. You go dancing with the rest of the group and stay out way past dawn. The next day you get a call from the president of the United States.

"The Syndrome, and you in particular, are the best ambassadors we've ever had," he says. "And the best thing is that the concert was broadcast over Soviet national TV. Nearly everyone in the Soviet Union watched it."

"I'm really glad to hear that, sir."

"I'll sign off now," the president says. "I don't want to run up the phone bill because we still have a serious budget problem here, but I did want to thank you, and let you know—you're a *super* superstar!"

The End

You realize that Steve is right. After a few days biking through the French countryside with friends, you feel like a new person. You can hardly wait to get to the French Open and play tennis.

From then on things go beautifully. You sweep through the tournament, and then, in the most thrilling moment of your career, you win at Wimbledon and find yourself shaking hands with the queen of England.

You're going for the Grand Slam! You're going to face Blair Caukins, the Australian who has dominated the game the last few years and is still the number-one player in the world. Blair didn't play in the Australian Open because he was recovering from knee surgery, but he's come back strong and is favored to win at the U.S. Open in September.

Blair is an awesome player and in the last few months has regained the form and stamina that produced what one sportscaster called "one of the most graceful, consistent, and powerful players the game has ever known."

As a friend of yours says, "I've never seen Blair let up for a minute. Blair is the closest thing to superhuman I've ever seen."

September. The U.S. Open, in Flushing Meadows, where sometimes you can't hear the ball hit the racket because of the roar of the jets taking off at La Guardia Airport.

Turn to page 105.

You could be a sports star, but you enjoy playing the piano so much that you don't have time for it. There are so many pieces of music you want to learn to play—not to mention the music you want to compose on your own. Your fingers always seem to know where to move on the keyboard, and the sound that comes out—well, put it this way: whoever is around usually ends up hanging over the piano, admiring you.

As your classical teacher, Sylvia Glinkhoff, says in her thick European accent, "You are a *wunderkind*. Beethoven himself would never be playing better."

And as your jazz coach, "88 Keys" Weston, says about the demo you made for Starlight Records, "You're what it's all about, kid."

You start going to classical concerts. You meet a number of famous musicians and get to play with the renowned cellist Michael Chang. That same day you're offered a full scholarship to the Philadelphia Conservatory. Then something happens that blows your socks off—a call from Tim Adriance, lead singer of The Syndrome, which just happens to be your favorite rock group. They want you to join them.

The deadline for the conservatory is only a few days away, and Tim needs an answer even sooner. What will you do?

If you decide to become a classical star, turn to page 115.

If you decide to become a rock star, turn to page 36.

112

You drive hard, taking the moguls one jump after another, gathering speed every time. You jump! *CRACK! You've hit a rock! Your right ski careens out of control. You're down!*

You can feel the pain running up your leg, but you're not ready to give up the race yet. You manage to get back on your feet somehow and fly wildly through the finish line where you collapse.

Turn to page 87.

Maybe one in a thousand people could grab the barrel of a rifle pointed at them and deflect it before it's fired. It's a pretty foolish thing to do—for most people. But you are different—you're a superstar!

You seize the barrel with a lightning stroke, sending the stock of the rifle into the face of the thug at the other end. He groans, releasing his grip. You yank out the rifle and turn it on the wheels of the limo as it starts off.

Crack! Crack! You flatten the left rear tire and send the limo skidding into a moving van.

Turn to page 106.

You decide to become a classical star and accept the scholarship at the conservatory. During the next few years you study under some of the greatest pianists in the world. Even before you graduate, you've won a list of music prizes a page long, including the famous Prokofiev competition in Moscow.

Then you're given an opportunity that is generally reserved for the greatest artists, a recital in Carnegie Hall in which you're accompanied by the New York Philharmonic. You start off with Mozart's Concerto No. 44 in B-flat and then play Bach's "Well-tempered Clavier."

The response is stunning: a 12-minute standing ovation, and words from the critics such as "unparalleled artistry," "a young master of enormous talent," "a celestial performance."

As far as you're concerned, the conductor, Serge Kandinsky, puts it better than anyone, as the two of you are walking off the stage after your fifth curtain call. Tapping your arm, he says, "You're a superstar, kid."

The End

ABOUT THE AUTHOR

EDWARD PACKARD is a graduate of Princeton University and Columbia Law School. He developed the unique storytelling approach used in the Choose Your Own Adventure series while thinking up stories for his children, Caroline, Andrea, and Wells.

ABOUT THE ILLUSTRATOR

STEPHEN MARCHESI graduated from Pratt Institute. He has illustrated many books for both children and adults. His drawings have also appeared in magazines, textbooks, and children's educational publications. Stephen Marchesi currently lives and works in Bayside, New York.

CHOOSE YOUR OWN ADVENTURE ®

- ☐ 27227   THE PERFECT PLANET #80 $2.50
- ☐ 27277   TERROR IN AUSTRALIA #81 $2.50
- ☐ 27356   HURRICANE #82 $2.50
- ☐ 27533   TRACK OF THE BEAR #83 $2.50
- ☐ 27474   YOU ARE A MONSTER #84 $2.50
- ☐ 27415   INCA GOLD #85 $2.50
- ☐ 27595   KNIGHTS OF THE ROUND TABLE #86 $2.50
- ☐ 27651   EXILED TO EARTH #87 $2.50
- ☐ 27718   MASTER OF KUNG FU #88 $2.50
- ☐ 27770   SOUTH POLE SABOTAGE #89 $2.50
- ☐ 27854   MUTINY IN SPACE #90 $2.50
- ☐ 27913   YOU ARE A SUPERSTAR #91 $2.50
- ☐ 27968   RETURN OF THE NINJA #92 $2.50
- ☐ 28009   CAPTIVE #93 $2.50

Choosy Kids Choose

CHOOSE YOUR OWN ADVENTURE ®

☐ 26157-6 JOURNEY TO THE YEAR 3000
Super Edition #1 $2.95

☐ 26791-4 DANGER ZONES Super Edition #2 $2.95

☐ 26965-5 THE CAVE OF TIME #1 $2.75

☐ 27393-0 JOURNEY UNDER THE SEA #2 $2.50

☐ 26593-8 DANGER IN THE DESERT #3 $2.50

☐ 27453-8 SPACE AND BEYOND #4 $2.50

☐ 27419-8 THE CURSE OF THE HAUNTED
MANSION #5 $2.50

☐ 23182-0 SPY TRAP #6 $2.50

☐ 23185-5 MESSAGE FROM SPACE #7 $2.50

☐ 26213-0 DEADWOOD CITY #8 $2.50

☐ 23181-2 WHO KILLED HARLOWE
THROMBEY? #9 $2.50

☐ 25912-1 THE LOST JEWELS #10 $2.50

☐ 27520-8 SPACE PATROL #22 $2.50

☐ 27053-2 VAMPIRE EXPRESS #31 $2.50